Things I Like

I Like to Dance

By Meg Gaertner

level 1 little blue readers

www.littlebluehousebooks.com

Little Blue House is distributed by North Star Editions:
sales@northstareditions.com | 888-417-0195

Produced for Little Blue House by Red Line Editorial.

Photographs ©: Yagi-Studio/iStockphoto, cover; twinsterphoto/iStockphoto, 4; SpeedKingz/Shutterstock Images, 6–7; vgajic/iStockphoto, 9; DisobeyArt/iStockphoto, 11, 16 (bottom right); BraunS/iStockphoto, 12–13, 16 (top right); rbv/iStockphoto, 15; Gilgatron/iStockphoto, 16 (top left); JackF/iStockphoto, 16 (bottom left)

Library of Congress Control Number: 2019908640

ISBN
978-1-64619-016-4 (hardcover)
978-1-64619-055-3 (paperback)
978-1-64619-094-2 (ebook pdf)
978-1-64619-133-8 (hosted ebook)

Printed in the United States of America
Mankato, MN
012020

About the Author

Meg Gaertner enjoys reading, writing, dancing, and being outside. She lives in Minnesota.

Table of Contents

I Like to Dance

I dance alone.

I listen to music.

I dance in a class.

We move the same way.

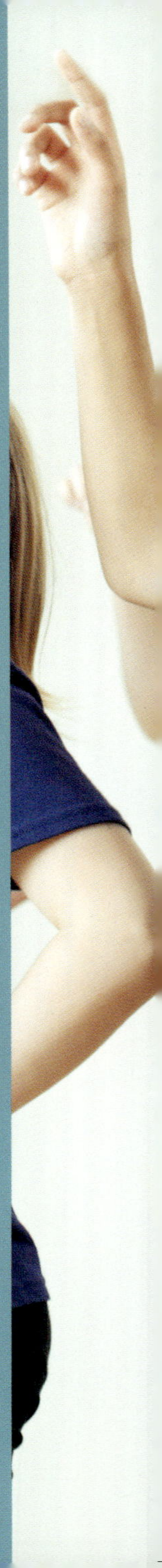

I dance ballet.

I point my toes.

I raise my arm.

arm
toes

I dance with my mom.
She spins me around.

mom

I dance with my dad.

He lifts me up.

dad

I lift my legs up.

I do a hard move.

leg

Glossary

ballet

dad

class

mom

Index